THE TIME MACHINE NEXT DOOR

EXPLORERS AND MILKSHAKES

ILLUSTRATED BY
REBECCA BAGLEY

ISZI LAWRENCE

BLOOMSBURY EDUCATION

LONDON OXFORD NEW YORK NEW DELHI SYDNEY

BLOOMSBURY EDUCATION
Bloomsbury Publishing Plc
50 Bedford Square, London, WC1B 3DP, UK
29 Earlsfort Terrace, Dublin 2, Ireland

BLOOMSBURY, BLOOMSBURY EDUCATION and the Diana logo are trademarks
of Bloomsbury Publishing Plc

First published in Great Britain in 2023 by Bloomsbury Publishing Plc

A catalogue record for this book is available from the British Library

ISBN: PB: 978-1-80199-104-9; ePDF: 978-1-80199-102-5; ePub: 978-1-80199-103-2

2 4 6 8 10 9 7 5 3 1

Typeset by Newgen KnowledgeWorks Pvt. Ltd., Chennai, India
Printed and bound by CPI Group (UK) Ltd, Croydon, CR0 4YY

To find out more about our authors and books visit www.bloomsbury.com
and sign up for our newsletters

THE TIME MACHINE NEXT DOOR

EXPLORERS AND MILKSHAKES

CONTENTS

For Noah

CHAPTER ONE

Sunil was in big trouble. **MASSIVE** trouble. The **BIGGEST** trouble any boy had ever been in.

He was panicking so much that he didn't notice the mattress on Alex's front lawn. It was a large one, and

took up nearly the entire front garden. Then again, why would he notice? Unlike all the other quiet semi-detached houses on their street, Alex's was the only one with scorch marks and lunar panels. There were already so many strange things about his neighbour and her house, like the electric windmill in her back garden and the time she set fire to her bathroom.

He had to be quick. He only had minutes before his parents would notice he'd snuck next door. He rang the doorbell with his free hand. The other sheltered a damaged record from the rain under his coat.

'Is she not in?' said a cool voice behind him.

Sunil's head whipped round. There, in Alex's front garden, stood the strangest man Sunil had ever seen. It wasn't just the man's pink umbrella, trendy trainers or colourful suit. Or his chunky glasses, blond goatee beard and curly hair

that reminded Sunil of broccoli.
What made him most peculiar was
the thing that was tucked under
his arm.

It could be
mistaken for a
small, fluffy,
brown cat until it
started sniffing
the air. The
snuffling
noises were
coming out of what

Sunil at first thought was a pencil. It was actually a long, curved beak. Beady eyes blinked curiously at Sunil from behind long black whiskers.

'Is that a kiwi?' Sunil asked, stepping closer.

The kiwi strained against the man's grip and sniffed at Sunil, pointing its beak into his collar.[1]

1. Kiwis have the smallest eyes (relative to their size) of all birds. They can't see very well and so they like to sniff things to learn about them.

It was almost like it could smell the record hidden in his jacket. Sunil could certainly smell the kiwi; it was musty like old socks.

The man bent over him. 'Are you an expert on kiwis?'

'No,' Sunil said. 'I just know the Kiwis is another name for the Black Caps, New Zealand's cricket team.'

At this the kiwi gave a dismissive huff and stopped sniffing him. Just then, there was a loud **THUD**. It came from above.

'Just a minute!' Alex's voice called.

Both Sunil and the stranger stepped back to see what was happening on the roof. Alex's face poked out over the guttering.

'Sunil!' She smiled and then scowled when she saw the stranger. 'I told you, I'm not interested, Mr Shaykes!'

'I only wanted to purchase some more objects,' Mr Shaykes began, but was stopped mid-sentence by Alex somersaulting off the roof.

8

She landed with a large squelch on the waterlogged mattress. The kiwi started to make **peeping** noises and, unable to reach Alex, started sniffing at Sunil again.

'Goodbye Mr Shaykes,' Alex said, pulling Sunil into the house.

'Let me know if you change your mind…'

'I won't!' she said, **SLAMMING** the door.

CHAPTER TWO

Alex looked nervously out of the peephole to make sure Mr Shaykes had left, then she turned to Sunil. 'Your parents didn't tell me you needed babysitting today.'

'I'm not a baby!' Sunil showed her the broken record in his jacket. 'I need your help.'

'Ah, so that is why Wiki was so interested in you,' Alex said, looking closely at the record.

'Wiki?'

'The kiwi,' Alex said. 'He's trained to sniff out interesting objects. Kiwis are the only birds to have their nostrils on the tips of their beaks.'

'Can you fix it?' Sunil asked, as Alex held two pieces together.

She shook her head. Sunil sat down on the floor. All hope was lost. His parents would never speak to him again.

'*Bad Moon Rising*?' Alex said. 'It's just an old record. Why is it so important?'[1]

---

1. *Bad Moon Rising* is a song by the band Creedence Clearwater Revival & John Fogerty which was released in April 1969. It sounds happy and jaunty but is actually about a forthcoming apocalypse (the end of the world)! It contains the line, "I feel the hurricane blowin', I hope you're quite prepared to die." Eeek! It was written during the Cold War when many people were worried they would die because of nuclear bombs.

'It's from when my nanabapa came to England,' he said. 'The first record he bought. He kept it on his shelf. And now Mum keeps it on our shelf. And I broke it…'

'We've got the fragments,' Alex said, holding up a piece of the record. 'Which means I can use its atoms to pinpoint its location in the timeline. Get that wrong and you

can end up anywhere. Last week,
I got stranded at sea.'

She pointed to a large fish tank in
the corner. It had a woolly hat on top
of it and a lobster inside.

She's gone mad, Sunil thought.

He followed Alex past towering
piles of wires and gizmos. In the
middle of the house, by the staircase,
was a large puddle of water. Sunil

looked up and realised that she had cut a skylight in her roof that wasn't all the way closed.

'I don't want to use the mattress every time,' Alex said, noticing his look. 'Before we go any further, you have to promise never to tell a word of this to anyone.'

Sunil wasn't paying attention; he'd picked up a piece of twisted metal from a pile and was playing with it.

Alex frowned. 'Swear that if you tell any other living soul, you will no longer support India at cricket. You'll be an England fan instead.'

Sunil looked up. He could imagine what his cousins would say if he began supporting England. Alex stood with her arms folded, waiting for him to agree.

'I swear,' Sunil said, putting the piece of metal into his pocket.

Alex beamed. She opened the door with a flourish. Inside was disappointing. On top of Alex's downstairs toilet there was an old filing cabinet with a lot of tubes and wires sticking out of it. There was a screen, some handles, and two drawers.

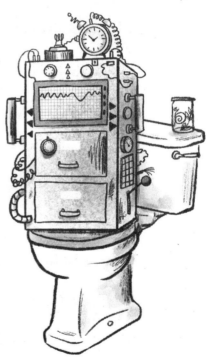

Sunil blinked. 'Can this repair the record?'

'Update complete,' said a computer voice. 'You look positive today.'

Alex blushed. 'I've programmed it to give me affirmations.'

'Your hair is shiny.'

'Thanks BM.' She started clicking different buttons and widgets. 'We don't need to repair the record if we can go back in time and get an exact copy. I've been wanting to tell people about BM for ages, but I haven't got it running perfectly yet.'

'You've invented a time machine?'

'I call it the Boring Machine. BM for short,' said Alex.

'I think you're marvellous,' the machine said.

'A Boring Machine?'

'You know how when you are really bored, time slows down?' Alex said.

'Yeah?'

'If time slows down when you're slightly bored,' she explained, 'then it will get slower still when you're super bored.'

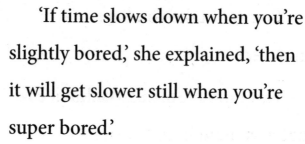

'When you are mega bored, time stops,' interrupted the machine. 'Nice shoes.'

'Thanks,' said Sunil.

Alex's eyes sparkled. 'I calculated that it is possible to be so bored that the clock doesn't just stop, it ticks backwards.'

'So can it take you back
anywhere you want?'

'Not quite. I need an old object
that was there in the past, like this.'
She placed the fragments of Sunil's
broken record into a drawer in
the side of the machine. 'It uses an
electron microscope to measure
the atoms to see where it has been.
Then, I feed the Boring Machine
something dull...'

She ran back out of the room and
came back with an old-fashioned

cassette tape. '... like a recording of
grown-ups talking about mortgages.'

'Yummy,' said the Boring
Machine as Alex placed it in a
different drawer.

'How do you get back?'
Sunil asked.

'The Boring Machine can't hold
you down in the past for too long.
If you get too excited your timeline
finds you and brings you back to the
present day.' She grinned. 'It feels like
it's pulling you by the belly button.'

'So, we aren't going to repair the record?'

'No, we'll go to a shop, buy another copy and be back here before you can say strawberry,' Alex said. 'Are your hands clean?'

'Yes,' Sunil said, wiping the grease from the scrap metal onto his jeans.

'Just make sure you don't let any clothing come into contact with the handles or it could follow that timeline instead of the record's. I'll get some peanuts.'

'Peanuts?'

'You'll need something salty,' Alex said, crossing the room and stuffing a packet of peanuts into her pocket. 'Peanuts, check. Lucky socks, check. Hold onto the handles. Try not to reach out when you land. Keep your arms tucked in or you could hurt your shoulders. Ready?'

Sunil felt like his entire body was yawning. It was like doing a backflip except he missed the floor. He spun back so fast that colours streaked

in front of him. Gradually it slowed
and the world assembled itself into a
completely different place.

CHAPTER THREE

Wind **ROARED** in Sunil's ears. He opened his eyes. Bright sunshine, blue sky, green and yellow fields. Sunil was falling. He was high over a strange flat landscape. Something invisible was tugging his belly button incredibly hard, like it was trying to lift him back up into the sky.

He was only a few hundred metres from the ground. Below him was a strip of tarmac and the noise of a thousand vacuum cleaners. He caught a glimpse of a giant piece of flying scaffolding, shaped like a wingless fly. It was a cross between a humongous drone and a climbing frame. At the front of it sat a man wearing a white helmet. The machine had changed direction and was fast approaching Sunil.

It all took less than a second.

Sunil reached out as the flying craft rose up to meet him. He landed in the lap of the pilot. They made eye contact and the whole machine lurched to the side. Sunil felt his belly button yank straight up. The pilot reached for a lever and there was a loud boom. The cockpit had exploded. Sunil was clear. He was being pulled upwards faster than he'd been falling. The colours blurred and he flipped forwards.

***

Wham. Sunil landed face down on what seemed to be a patio. He coughed and sat up. There was an American flag hanging limp on a flagpole. The sky was threatening to rain. He could hear traffic and a crowd of people somewhere below him. He was on a roof.

Overlooking the edge of the roof was a giant statue of an eagle. Sunil steadied himself by touching its enormous golden wing and looked down below. About five storeys beneath him there was a large group of people dispersing on the steps. Men were packing up cameras and signalling for black cabs.

Black cabs. They didn't have those in America, did they? He looked back up at the flag and caught sight of a man on the other side of the statue, also looking down at the crowd. He was dressed in black and had a gun. Sunil hesitated.

'Excuse me?'

The man with the gun nearly leapt out of his skin and turned towards Sunil.

'Where am I?'

'**FREEZE!**' shouted the man.

Sunil felt a tug on his belly button. *Oh no, not again.* He needed to get inside if he didn't want to get pulled up into the sky.

'Hands up!'

Sunil ran behind the flagpole and spotted the entrance to a stairwell. He dashed for it, terrified the man would start shooting. He clattered down the metal steps and launched himself through a door and into a corridor. He walked quickly underneath the buzzing fluorescent lights, double checking that the man from the roof wasn't following him.

The corridor wasn't empty. There were women with their hair up, wearing short skirts and men in ties smoking cigarettes. They all had American accents and were giving him confused glances.

Sunil rounded a corner and found himself in a large open

room where dozens of women were sitting furiously jabbing at typewriters. On the wall there was a sign saying 'secretarial pool' and another American flag. No one was swimming.

He needed to find Alex.

He didn't know her number but he did know he could reach her on a messaging app that his family used. He just needed to borrow someone's phone and download it. He walked up to the desk closest to him.

'Excuse me, I'm lost.'

'Oh, Sweetie! What can I do to help?'

'Can I borrow your phone?'

'You can use this one.' The woman indicated the large black Bakelite telephone with a circular dial.

'I need a mobile,' Sunil said.

She stared at him blankly. 'Mobile?'

'Your cell?' He tried miming one. 'I need to download a messaging app.'

'Are you OK, Hun?'

Just then a man came in and stood behind Sunil.

'Can I help you, Lieutenant?' asked the woman.

Sunil turned round and locked eyes with the blond man standing behind him.

'You!' the man gasped.

Sunil also recognized him immediately. He was the pilot of the bizarre flying drone he had landed

on moments ago. He felt a giant tug
at his belly button.

'Oh, do you know him?' The
secretary beamed. 'The poor boy is
lost. Can you help him?'

The blond man blinked and
grabbed Sunil by the wrist. 'I
sure can.'

Sunil was dragged out of the
secretarial pool and straight into
a stationery cupboard. The blond
man turned on the light and shut the
door behind him.

CHAPTER FOUR

'You're real?!' The man patted Sunil
on the head. 'I knew I wasn't mad!
I lied and said the LLRV controls
stopped working.'

'LLRV?' Sunil repeated.

'Lunar Landing Research Vehicle.
I had to eject after I lost control.
When they didn't find your body,
I assumed you'd been vaporised.'

'Sorry about that,' Sunil said.

'I'm happy you're alive! You can
tell people what really happened.'

'I don't know what happened.
I was supposed to be travelling with
my friend Alex. I need to find her.'

The man's eyes glimmered in
recognition. 'Is Alex a woman with
coloured bits in her hair, wearing a

green boiler suit and a t-shirt with a banana on it?'

'Yes!' Sunil said in relief. 'Do you know where she is?'

'Getting arrested last I saw. Come on!'

They left the cupboard and made their way back down the corridor. Sunil noticed that the people weren't looking at him anymore. Everyone was beaming at the blond man. Sunil was invisible next to him.

When they got into the elevator, Sunil whispered to him, 'Why is everyone looking at you like that?'

'Like what?'

'Like you're famous.'

'I've only been here a few hours,' the man explained. 'It takes time for folks to get used to you.'

'Are you famous?'

He laughed. 'Geez kid, you know how to bring a guy back down to Earth.'

The elevator stopped and they exited on a different corridor. Unlike on the floor above, everyone on this corridor was male and in military uniform.

They stopped by a soldier guarding a plain looking door.

'Hi, Sergeant.'

'Sir.' The guard couldn't control his smile.

'Can you do me a favour? I want to speak to the Soviet spy,' the man said.[1]

---

1. People from the Soviet Union (also known as the Union of Soviet Social Republics or the USSR) were called Soviets. Russia took over lots of Eastern Europe after the Second World War and formed the USSR. The USA and USSR didn't like each other. They were like squabbling siblings and tried to outdo each other with who had the best athletes or bigger bombs. They both wanted to be first to put a man in space (USSR won) and to put a man on the Moon (USA won).

'That's not really…' The guard paused and whispered, 'Can I get your autograph, Sir? My wife would be amazed I met you.'[2]

'Deal,' the man said. 'Me and the boys had to sign a truck load

2. Before people carried cameras on their mobile phones, they couldn't easily take selfies with famous people. To prove they'd met them they would get them to sign their name in an autograph book. Stationers actually printed special blank notebooks for this purpose!

of random stuff already. One more can't hurt.'

He wrote something in the guard's notebook while the guard unlocked the door.

Alex was sitting alone in a windowless office.

'Sunil!' she squeaked happily. 'I thought I'd lost you!'

He ran to her, giving her a big hug. She looked up at the man he'd come in with and her mouth gaped open.

'Neil Armstrong!'[3]

'Ma'am.'

Sunil cocked his head, something about the name was familiar.

'You must know who he is!' spluttered Alex.

Sunil shook his head apologetically.

3. Neil Armstrong (1930-2012). As a kid, he had travel sickness but he learnt to fly a plane when he was 16 years old. That was before he learned to drive a car!

'He was the first man to land on the…' Alex stopped. 'Sorry, what is the date?'

'October 14th,' Neil said.

'The year?'

'1969.'

'Fab. Neil Armstrong was the first man to walk on the Moon,' Alex said.

'What's wrong, kid?'

'You're old,' Sunil said.[4]

'Sunny!' Alex said.

'In school they said the astronauts were fighter pilots.'

'I was yes,' Neil said. 'But that was during the Korean War. Now I'm a test pilot.'[5]

4. 39 – really old!
5. Neil Armstrong was a pilot in the US air force in the Korean War in the 1950s.

'And astronaut,' said Sunil.[6]

Neil looked embarrassed. 'Oh yes, that too.'

'Are you in England to meet the Queen?'

6. Neil Armstrong went to the Moon in the Apollo 11 spacecraft with his crewmates Edward E "Buzz" Aldrin and Michael Collins. Only Neil and Buzz got to walk on the surface of the Moon. When Neil landed the lunar module, there were only thirty seconds of fuel left. They used a different engine to take off and meet up with Michael who was orbiting the Moon in the Apollo command module.

'Part of the 22-stop world tour,' Neil said, nodding. 'And I've already got a cold.[7] Listen, I want to know how this little boy landed on my LLRV last year, nearly killing me. Was it Soviet sabotage?'[8]

7. All the Apollo astronauts had stinking colds when they were in London to meet the Queen and Prime Minister!

8. A year before he set foot on the Moon, Neil Armstrong nearly died in an LLRV (Lunar Landing Research Vehicle) crash at an air force base in Houston, Texas. Grown-ups want you to believe that this wasn't because of a time traveller but you can make your own decision about that...

'Last year? That happened twenty minutes ago!'

'That's right!' Alex was holding her forehead to keep her eyebrows from raising too high. 'Neil Armstrong nearly died the year before the Moon landings. I actually have some of the metal from that crash! I swapped it for a pterosaur neck fossil… Oh no!'

Alex turned to Sunil. 'Did you touch anything in my house before we left?'

Sunil reached into his pocket and produced the twisted piece of scrap metal he'd been fidgeting with in Alex's house.

Her eyes widened. 'Of course! Look at the grease on your hands!'

'I wiped them off before touching the handles.' Sunil said.

'Not well enough! I bet that stuff got on the Boring Machine and confused it. I'll make a note to insulate the handles in future.'

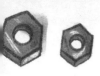

'A what machine?' asked Neil Armstrong.

'It's this rudimentary time machine I'm testing. It gets confused easily. It must have followed the timeline of the grease from your LLRV accident, not the timeline of the *Bad Moon Rising* record.'

Neil Armstrong opened and closed his mouth a few times, as if trying to work out what question to ask first.

'But why did it take us here?' Alex said. 'This is the American Embassy in London, not a record shop.'

'They'll never believe me,' Neil said, putting his head in his hands.

'The record must be here somewhere,' Sunil said. 'If the Boring Machine follows the timeline of objects…'

'I am sick of that song,' Neil said. 'Everyone plays it for us because it

has the word 'moon' in it. We get given loads of copies to sign.'

'You do? What happens to them?'

Neil shrugged. 'They get donated to charity or sold on to record shops.'

'That's why we're here!' Alex said to Sunil. 'The record is here somewhere. It must get sold on and your Grandad will buy it second hand!'

'That sounds like him. Wait!' Sunil's belly button tugged again and he turned to Neil Armstrong. 'You said there was a whole truckload of stuff that you had to autograph. Were there any copies of the record there?'

'Probably. I've been asked to sign everything from a man's forehead to a rubber duck. If it were my choice, I wouldn't sign anything. I'm not special, they could have picked someone else to go to the Moon,' Neil Armstrong said, frowning. 'If it wasn't me, it would have been another guy.'

'But it wasn't another guy,'
Sunil said. 'It was you.'[9]

'We're running out of time,'
Alex said, her hand pressing on her
stomach. Sunil could feel something
tugging on his belly button too.
'Sorry Neil, big fan, but if you
could show us where the stuff you
signed is...'

9. The footprints made by Neil Armstrong
and Buzz Aldrin on the Moon are still there!
There is no wind to blow them away.

'Technically, I'm a civilian. I have no authority to take you out of this room.'

'Yeah, but you're Neil Armstrong!'

Chapter Five

Sure enough, a few winks and handshakes were the magic access code to much of the building. No one questioned that Neil Armstrong had taken custody of a suspected Soviet spy. He marched them to the office where he had been signing autographs.[1]

The room was packed with posters, photographs and random objccts. Sunil and Alex ransacked the piles, looking for a copy of the record. Neil kept a lookout by the door. Sunil got distracted by some coins on the floor.

1. Six hundred million people watched the Moon landing live on TV and even more listened to it on the radio. Neil Armstrong was REALLY famous!

'That's a thrupenny bit. A three pence coin,' Alex said knowingly. 'Britain didn't change to metric coins until 1971.'

'What's this one?' Sunil turned it over in his hand. 'It has a little ship on the back.'

'That's a ha'penny,' Alex said. 'Oooh, it's old. Minted in 1910.'[2]

Sunil looked disappointed. 'Will it buy anything?'

2. In 'old money' there were 240 pennies in a pound because King Henry II based the value of money on the weight of the coins. The original penny coin was made of silver and 240 of them weighed a pound! (Good thing he didn't use the metric weight system or we would have to call pound coins, 453.6 gram coins!)

'Half a penny sweet? Oh!'

Alex had found a stack of records. 'There are six copies! All identical.'

Sunil ran over. A wave of relief washed over him. He had his record.

Sunil felt a harsh tug at his belly button. They were being slowly pulled upward.

'What's happening?' Neil Armstrong said. 'Your hair is standing up.'

'We need to get outside,' Alex said.

'There is a fire escape at the end of the corridor.'

Sunil and Alex ran past women in thick rimmed spectacles and men with strange haircuts. Sunil felt his feet lift off the ground. Something behind his belly button was yanking incredibly hard. Just as they fell through the door Sunil's body rose up. He caught sight of the London skyline. There was a great

WHOOSHING in his ears.

Everything went black.[3]

***

Sunil blinked. He was on Alex's roof.

3. There isn't a sensible place to put this fact but I thought you'd like to know that in 1985 Neil Armstrong travelled to the North Pole with the first European man to climb Mount Everest – Sir Edmund Hillary. They flew there in a small plane and when they opened some champagne to celebrate... it froze! On their way back they got stuck in a white-out snowstorm and while they were waiting for it to clear they swapped stories of their adventures.

Alex sat up next to him, panting. 'Please tell me you still have the record.'

Sunil held it up. His arms were shaking.

They climbed down through Alex's skylight.

'Remember, don't tell anyone anything,' Alex said. 'You'd best hurry; we're late getting back.'

Sunil didn't have long. He ran through Alex's kitchen to the fence in the back garden. There was a loose panel and he snuck through it and ran up his garden to the back door. Tara, their dog, **BARKED** loudly. His mum was in her study and didn't notice him sneaking into the living room. He put the record back on the shelf. The front door **SLAMMED**.

'I'm home!'

'Dad!' Sunil ran into the hallway and gave his father the biggest hug. The wobbly feeling of being flung through space and time evaporated.

'Hey, Sunny, are you alright?'

Sunil nodded but kept squeezing. He had never felt more grounded.

His dad ruffled his hair. 'How about you and I go for a lad's treat? Fancy a milkshake?'

'A milkshake?'

'There's a new place on the corner,' Sunil's dad said.

CHAPTER SIX

The café was only down the road, next to the newsagents and the chip shop. It looked like a cartoon. Tara sniffed the colourful 'pets welcome' sign. If Sunil thought the place was bright on the outside, the inside was like a box of crayons. Neon signs flickered on psychedelic walls and screens flashed adverts for milkshake meal combos. Behind the glass counter were buckets of toppings.

A girl in an orange apron and bright pink beret slumped by the register. In a monotonous tone she said, 'Welcome to Mr Shaykes's Milkshake Emporium. Our milkshake maker uses the latest technology to provide you

with the best tasting milkshake in Manchester. Tell us an interesting fact and we will provide you with the ultimate beverage experience.'

Sunil's dad looked confused. 'You don't do chocolate or banana?'

'Each milkshake is tailored by the Interesting Machine to the fact you provide,' the girl continued. 'The more fascinating the fact, the more delicious the drink.'

'An Interesting Machine?' Sunil frowned.

'It takes your facts and mixes them into milkshakes,' the girl said in an annoyed tone, as though she regularly had this argument.

'What sort of fact?' Sunil asked.

'It's up to you.'

'Um… the first cricket world cup was in 1975?' Sunil's dad offered.

The girl turned her nose up. 'The machine doesn't like sport. It broke down when someone listed golfing tournaments. It literally cried.'

'Oh.' Dad looked embarrassed. 'Are you sure you don't have strawberry?'

'How about: the kiwi is the only bird to have its nostrils on the end of its beak?' Sunil offered.

The teenager squinted suspiciously at him. 'That's a good one.'

'How did you get here so fast?' said a voice behind Sunil.

Sunil jumped. It was the man he had seen at Alex's house earlier. Mr Shaykes. He was panting.

'Oh wow!' Sunil's dad peered at the kiwi in Mr Shaykes's arms. 'What a coincidence! Is that a kiwi?'

Tara started to growl.

'This is Mr Shaykes, our CEO,'
the girl said.[1]

'You were right Sunil; it does
have nostrils at the end of its beak,'
Sunil's dad said.

Wiki snuffled through Sunil's
hair making excited **peeping** noises.

1. CEO means Chief Executive Officer
and is the swankiest of all job titles in an
organisation. Companies prefer CEO to 'Big
Boss' because otherwise too many video
gamers try to defeat them.

'It likes you!' Sunil's dad said. Tara continued to grumble.

'Why don't I show you how our milkshakes are made?' Mr Shaykes offered.

'Great!'

'I'm sorry we can't allow pets back there – health and safety,' Mr Shaykes said, gesturing to Tara.

'Oh.' Sunil's dad looked disappointed. 'But what about the kiwi?'

'Wiki is an employee.'

'You go, Sunil. It will be fun.'

Wiki scrambled up Sunil's jumper, his long claws scratching as he went. He **peeped** constantly.

'Ow!'

Sunil followed Mr Shaykes behind the counter and through the back door into the kitchen.

'This is where the magic happens,' said Mr Shaykes.

CHAPTER SEVEN

The contrast between the **fun, zany** milkshake bar and the **GREY, POORLY LIT** kitchen was stark. Most of the room was taken up by a large machine. It hummed and grumbled and whirred and chugged.

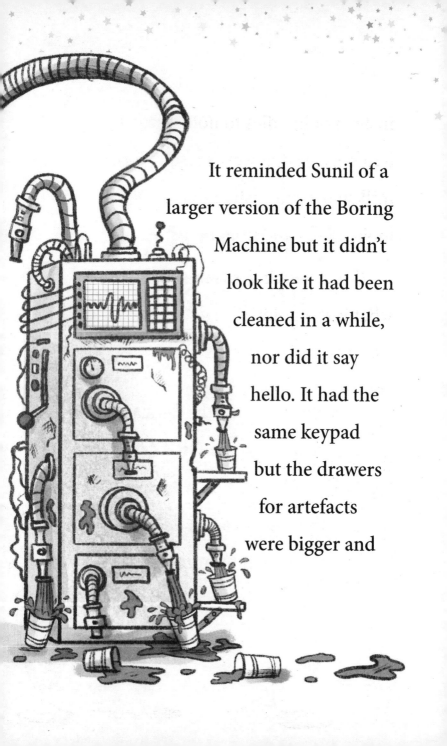

It reminded Sunil of a larger version of the Boring Machine but it didn't look like it had been cleaned in a while, nor did it say hello. It had the same keypad but the drawers for artefacts were bigger and instead of handles to hold onto, it had nozzles that were spewing out milkshakes into paper cups. They looked grey and unappetising.

'We're taught facts in school, but what is the point? I've given them a use! The Interesting Machine turns your facts into milkshakes,' Mr Shaykes said, taking a swig of one of the milkshakes and pulling a face. 'The only downside is that if you use old facts it tastes like onions.'

'Can't you make stuff up?'

'I tried that. Fake facts taste great but they poison everyone.' Mr Shaykes scratched his head. 'The problem is, my customers don't know enough good facts. Getting exciting information is really hard. There is a drawer where I can put whole books in, but the machine doesn't like reading.'

The machine grunted.

Sunil looked over at the window where there were stacks of old books on everything. They were stacked

by title from *Antarctic Explorers* to *Zebra Sleeping Habits*.[1]

'Interesting things make the best milkshakes,' Mr Shaykes continued. 'According to Wiki, you are the **MOST INTERESTING** thing he has ever come across.'

1. The Arctic is at the north of the planet and is home to polar bears. The Antarctic is at the south of the plant and is full of ants... I mean penguins. I don't know why they named it after ants. Do you?

'Me?' said Sunil.

'It doesn't make any sense, because when we met at Alex's house you were just a normal kid. So, what happened in the last hour to make you the **MOST INTERESTING** person on the planet?'

Sunil remembered his promise to Alex and shrugged.

'You will make some very good milkshakes.' Mr Shaykes opened the

drawer in the side of the machine.
'Get in.'

'I'm not interesting!' Sunil said,
but Mr Shaykes made a grab for him.

Sunil backed away. Wiki's claws
dug into his shoulder.

'It probably won't kill you,' Mr
Shaykes said. 'It will just suck all the
INTERESTING things out of
you. Then you'll be left as a normal
boring kid.'

Sunil bumped into the counter
behind him. To his left, the kitchen

door was shut. The back door was propped open on the other side of the Interesting Machine but Mr Shaykes's thin legs were blocking Sunil's way. He reached up and plucked Wiki from his shoulder. The bird was a lot thinner than his fluff made him seem. Sunil threw him high in the air. Mr Shaykes stopped in his tracks to catch the terrified **peeping** kiwi. Sunil charged between Mr Shaykes's bandy legs like he was trying to dive to catch a cricket ball.

He skidded across the tiles, bumping into the Interesting Machine. The half-made oniony milkshakes fell to the ground, splattering everywhere.[2]

'Come back!' Mr Shaykes shouted as Sunil sped out of the back door.

2. The state vegetable of Texas is the sweet onion.

CHAPTER EIGHT

Sunil ran past the bins and out into the car park. He dodged between the cars and hid behind a large white van. Looking back, he waited for Mr Shaykes to come out. No sign. Sunil breathed a sigh of relief.

Then he heard snuffling. Wiki had followed him out and, when he found him, started **peeping** like a policeman's whistle. The back door burst open and Mr Shaykes appeared, carrying what looked to Sunil like a pool net and a broom. The kiwi peeped again, calling Mr Shaykes to Sunil's hiding place. He had no choice but to run.

To Sunil's horror, the kiwi sped after him. He was as fast as Sunil and kept **peeping** for Mr Shaykes to follow. Sunil sprinted out of the car park, down a small alley and back into his street where he bumped head first into Alex.

'Sunil!' she said in surprise, but when she saw Wiki her eyes widened.

'It's Mr Shaykes!' Sunil panted. 'He wants to turn me into milkshakes!'

To Sunil's relief, Alex didn't stop to ask questions. She dropped her shopping bag, grabbed his arm and ran.

They sped down the street, pursued by the bird and Mr Shaykes. Passers-by took out their phones to film them.

Then there was a **BOOM**. It shook the ground. Mr Shaykes stopped, but the kiwi continued to chase Sunil and Alex.

'Hurry!' Alex said, pulling Sunil down a side alley. They turned down

a footpath that ran past the back of their houses. The **peeps** of the kiwi weren't far behind. Sunil could see the top of the electric windmill in the back of Alex's garden.

Alex stopped by the neighbour's wheelie bins and gave Sunil a key. 'Get in the house and start up BM. I'll be with you in two shakes of a lamb's tail.'

She helped Sunil climb up onto the wheelie bins. Wiki tried to follow but Alex grabbed him and continued to run with him down the alley. Sunil clambered over the garden fence. It wobbled as he dropped down into Alex's back garden. He battled through the brambles by the large wind turbine and unlocked her back door.[1] He knocked over a pile of engineering manuals as he came into the kitchen.

He went straight to the Boring Machine and began pressing buttons and switches in a panic.

1. Brambles grow super fast — even up to 8 cm in a day. So don't judge Alex on her untidy garden. She's a busy inventor after all.

'You look pretty with brambles in your hair,' it said. 'Please deposit your object.'

'I don't have a historical object!' Sunil said. 'I'm waiting for Alex.'

'Deposit your object or the system will close down for an update.'

'No,' Sunil said. 'Please stay on.'

'System will power down unless an object is deposited.'

Sunil felt around in his pockets and found the ha'penny.[2] 'Here.'

2. The ha'penny wasn't the smallest coin in old money. A farthing was worth half a ha'penny (one quarter of one pence). It stopped being used in mainland Britain in 1961 because it was worth so little. On the back was a picture of a wren, Britain's smallest native bird (it was the only one they could fit on the coin). The word farthing means 'four-thing' or 'quarter' in Old English.

'Hold onto the handles please.'

'But I haven't given you the coordinates...' Sunil said.

'Automatic system override.'

'Wait!'

'Hold onto the handles please.'

There was a **peep** by the back door; it was Wiki.

'Do it now!' Sunil said, grabbing the handles.

He felt himself spin backwards.

CHAPTER NINE

Sunil landed in bright white. It
was cold. Super cold. The air hurt
his lungs. His entire body started
trembling. The Boring Machine was
supposed to send him to a point
on an object's timeline. How could

the coin be here in the freezing nothingness? As his eyes adjusted to the whiteness, he saw a crane set against the white–blue sky.

He got up and stumbled towards it. His feet ached in the cold. Each step hurt as they quickly became encased in the powdery snow. The ground was uneven. Great lumps of ice the size of cars blocked his view.

There was a noise that sounded like barking. Sunil was bent over and could barely balance as he came over

the crest of ice. The crane turned out
to be the mast of a ship. It wasn't in
a dock or even on the ocean. It was
stuck fast in the ice, tilting over on its
side. Surrounding the ship was a camp
of tents and in front of the tents was a
nearly naked man sitting waist deep in
the snow pretending to have a bath.[1]

1. This is a true story. Captain Frank Worsely
was trying to give his crew a laugh by
bathing in ice because they had the blues
from being stuck. It worked. They had a
good laugh and, in the end, it was only
Frank's fingers and toes that were blue.

Surrounding him were about fifteen bearded men, all fully clothed laughing their heads off.

The man bathing in the snow spotted Sunil, jumped up in surprise and ripped the hat off his head and used it to cover himself.

'Who the devil are you?!' he exclaimed.

Sunil wasn't sure what happened next. Had he fainted or just slipped? The men rushed to him,

picking him up and putting a hat on his head. When he came to, they were running with him towards the ship. He was **trembling** uncontrollably.

'Take him to Mrs Chippy's tent. There's room in there.'

He was carried past crates and boxes laid out on the snow. Then he felt the warmth engulf him as they entered a tent. An oil lantern hung from the tent roof and one of the men lit it while the other placed Sunil on a

camp bed piled high with blankets. He was still shaking as they took off his jumper and trainers and rubbed his hands and feet.

'Did he stow away with Perce?'[2] one of the men said.

2. Eighteen-year-old Welshman, Perce Blackborow, stowed away on the ship *Endurance* when it docked in Buenos Aires (in Argentina). Shackleton was angry when they first discovered him aboard. He threatened Perce that if they ran out of food on the expedition, they would eat him first. Blackborow replied, "They'd get a lot more meat off you, sir." Which everyone found funny and so he joined the crew.

'Can't have; we'd have found him before now.'

'I'll find him some boots and a coat. You get him some tea.'

One of the men grunted and went outside while the other looked through an open crate. He offered Sunil an adult-sized coat and massive leather boots.

'Mrs Chippy has some sardines somewhere if you're hungry.'

'Who is Mrs Chippy?' Sunil asked, placing his feet in the boots, which fell back off before he could tie them.

The man started to make kissing sounds while looking around at the floor.

'He's here somewhere!'

'Mrs Chippy is a he?' Sunil asked.

'He's the carpenter's cat. Chippy is a nickname for a carpenter, and he and McNish have been inseparable, like husband and wife, ever since he found him on the London docks.'

The man called McNish returned
with a mug of warm tea. He handed
it to Sunil, who held it rather than
drank it, enjoying the warmth
spreading through his fingers.

'No sign of Mrs Chippy?'
McNish asked.

'Perhaps he's gone out?' Sunil
suggested.

'Out?! We're a hundred miles
from the South Pole!' McNish
looked worried. 'A cat won't last five
minutes out there.'

'We're at the South Pole?!' Sunil gasped.

'Where did you think we were?' The other man cocked his head. 'Do you know who I am?'

Sunil shook his head.

'Does exposure cause amnesia?' the man asked his friend.

McNish huffed loudly. 'He's Sir Ernest Shackleton, yer numbskull.'[3]

'I reckon Mrs Chippy's gone back to the ship,' Shackleton said.

3. Sir Ernest Shackleton was beaten to the South Pole by Norwegian Roald Amundsen in 1911. But he wanted to go back! So, he and 27 men set sail in 1914. They wanted to set the record by being the first people to walk across the continent... which seems like a lot of effort when they could just have decided to be the first people to dance the tango or play a tennis match there.

'If Mrs Chippy is on the ship, I'll go get him.'

Shackleton put out a hand to stop McNish. 'You can't, it is too dangerous. Your weight could cause the ship to shift in the ice and trap you inside. The water could rush in and drown you.'

'I'm not leaving Mrs Chippy!' McNish said angrily.[4]

'I'm much lighter than you. I'll find him,' Sunil offered.

4. Mrs Chippy was a real cat and he and McNish were inseparable.

118

CHAPTER TEN

Sunil regretted his offer the moment
he stepped back outside the tent.
They had encased him in McNish's
woolly hat, mittens, the thick adult
coat and large boots but the cold
clawed at him. He was starting to

shiver again, and the familiar pull of his belly button started the moment they reached the ship.

They approached from the rear. It looked less like a ship close up. It was tilted on its port side, so that some of it was submerged in the ice. Only some of the name on the stern was visible above the ice: *ndurance*. They walked to the side of the ship. Above was a tangle of rigging dangling from the masts. 'Mrs Chippy likes to sleep in the smoking

room, opposite the captain's cabin at the stern,' McNish said.

Sunil looked to where he was pointing. The deck glistened with ice. Reaching the door to the cabins was going to be tricky, particularly in oversized snow boots and mittens.

The moment he jumped down onto the deck he fell over. It was so slippery. He heard McNish giggle, but Shackleton shouted words of encouragement. He grabbed onto the frozen rigging and hauled

himself up to standing. He didn't
feel so cold anymore. He reached for
the door, lost his footing and gently
SLID back down the icy deck.

He laughed along with the
others but stopped when he heard a
strange, snapping echo. It sounded
alien. Sunil felt the tugging on his
belly button as his heartbeat sped up.

'Don't worry; it's just the ice,'
Shackleton said.

'It sounds like someone firing
lasers!' Sunil said.

'What are lasers?' Shackleton cocked his head.

There was another loud, pinging **CRACK**.

'What is that noise?'

'The sea water below moves the ice and it **CRACKS** and rises…' Shackleton explained.

'… and crushes the ship,' McNish said.

'How did it get stuck?' asked Sunil.

'My error. We travelled too far south,' Shackleton said. 'Sea ice froze around us. We were hoping the ice would thaw and release us.'[1]

'We've been stuck for ten months,' McNish said bitterly.

1. *Endurance* got stuck in the ice on January 18th 1915. They didn't abandon ship until October 27th 1915. *Endurance* finally sank on November 21st 1915. The crew escaped with three lifeboats and limited supplies but that was only the start of their adventure!

Sunil concentrated more on his second attempt. He kept hold of the frozen rope through his mittens and climbed carefully back up the deck. When he was alongside the open door, he made a leap for it. He caught hold of the door. His belly button started urgently tugging but he calmed himself down and pulled himself into the dark corridor.

'Mrs Chippy?' he called, making the same kissing noises to call her as Shackleton had back in the tent.

He saw something moving at the far end of the lopsided corridor. He hauled himself inside and began shuffling along with one boot on the floor the other on the wall.

There was another cracking noise and the boat shifted. He slammed into the wall.

'You alright?' Shackleton called.

'I'm fine!' Sunil yelled back.

He reached the end of the corridor and saw the cat, wide eyed, huddled under some fallen boxes by the narrow door. He looked bedraggled; there were ice flecks clinging to his whiskers.

'Hello, Mrs Chippy.'

Sunil offered the cat his hand, still encased in the mitten. Mrs Chippy gave it a sniff. Just as Sunil was about to stroke him, the boat shifted again and the outside door swung shut. Mrs Chippy hissed.

The tug on Sunil's belly button was getting more urgent. 'Please, we have to be quick!'

But the cat backed further away. Sunil pulled himself up through the doorframe into the smoking room. The ship groaned again. He felt the vibration of the metal beneath him buckling under the jaws of ice.

Mrs Chippy was backed up against the far wall. His tail was thrashing and he was hissing a warning for Sunil to back off. Sunil

took off his large coat to throw it over the animal. Mrs Chippy seemed to understand what was happening and bolted for the door. Sunil seized his moment and, without pausing to think, he dropped down onto the tabby cat like it was a rugby ball. Mrs Chippy hissed and screeched. Sunil had him upside down wrapped in the thick coat with his head under his arm and back legs squished against his stomach. Sunil jumped back out into the corridor, still clutching Mrs Chippy who was making a slow rumbling noise similar to the twisting metal beneath them.

Sunil was worried he might be hurting Mrs Chippy, but he couldn't risk letting the cat go in case he ran away again. His overly large shoes were difficult to walk in and as he came to the outside door, one fell off. He didn't go back for it; instead, he sat down outside of the door, held onto the coat and slid down the deck towards Shackleton and McNish.

'You'll freeze! Where is your shoe?'

'Why did you take your coat off?'

Mrs Chippy is in the coat!' Sunil said, standing up to hand it over.

After handing McNish the cat, Shackleton reached for Sunil and picked him up, swinging him onto his back.

'Good Lad,' he said, and walked him back to Mrs Chippy's tent.

They ducked into the tent, the wind billowing the walls. Mrs Chippy jumped onto the camp bed and curled up in a ball. Sunil stood awkwardly; when he had slid down the deck of the boat his jeans got wet and had now refrozen. Seeing the boy's discomfort, McNish told him to take them off and sit under a blanket. Sunil sat next to Mrs Chippy on the bed and gently stroked the soft fur behind his ears.

McNish sat on the other side and did the same.

'Pity about the shoe,' Shackleton said. 'Fortunately, we have several spare pairs. I suppose that is less for us to carry.'

'Carry?' Sunil asked.

'Yes, we have to get to land before the ice melts,' Shackleton explained. 'We can't take everything with us.'

At this point, McNish burst into tears.

'It's terribly sad,' Shackleton said softly. 'We're going to have to walk miles to get to safety. You've seen the conditions. We have to carry the lifeboats, with all our camping gear and food. We can only take the bare minimum. We can't take the cat.'

'Mrs Chippy!' McNish sobbed, burying his face in the cat's fur.

To Sunil it seemed a hopeless situation. It had nearly killed him walking fifty yards over the ice. They needed to walk miles. Carrying lifeboats and all their tents.

McNish sniffed and petted Mrs Chippy. 'The chances of us surviving are tiny. Why should I leave my only friend to die alone? I should be here with him.'

'Won't anyone rescue you? Don't you have a radio?' Sunil asked.

Shackleton shrugged. 'No one can reach us until the ice melts… and by then it will be too late.'

'It's too late anyway,' McNish said.

Shackleton looked nervous. 'It isn't. I will get you home.'

CHAPTER ELEVEN

'He's right! You will get home,' Sunil
said determinedly. 'I know you will.'

'I wish I had your faith, laddy.'
McNish shook his head.

'It's science not faith!' Sunil smiled. 'See this coin?'

He reached into his pocket and handed Shackleton the thrupenny bit he'd picked up from the embassy.[1] 'Look at the date.'

1. The thrupenny bit was worth three old pence. They started making them in 1547. Initially they were unpopular because people preferred the groat which was worth 4 pence. However, because both three and four fit really well into 240 (which was how many pence a pound was worth) it soon caught on.

'1937…' Shackleton held it up to the oil lamp.

McNish took and examined it.

'That coin was on the floor of the American Embassy in London in 1969. It's real.'

Shackleton looked at him dumbfounded.

'Where do you think I came from?' Sunil said with a wide grin on his face. 'I haven't been stowed away on your boat. I'm a time traveller. I'm only here because of another

coin I found alongside that one. I followed its timeline here.'

'You're a very imaginative boy,' Shackleton said.

'Someone in your crew has a halfpenny that will be in London in 1969 for me to pick up. I couldn't have found it there if it had stayed here, could I?'

Shackleton looked again closely at the thrupenny bit, trying to find fault with it.

'Where did he come from?' McNish whispered to Shackleton.

'In those thin clothes…' Shackleton murmured.

'You don't have to believe me,' Sunil said. He was getting excited and could feel his belly button tugging. 'Just let me save Mrs Chippy.'

'How?' Shackleton asked.

'Let me take him to the future!' Sunil said. 'If I could take a record and coins from 1969, why can't I take a cat to the 21st century?'

There was another loud pinging **CRACK**.

The tugging at Sunil's belly button was getting stronger.

'Is it possible that we're hallucinating?' Shackleton asked McNish.

'I don't know but it's worth a go, isn't it? If he can save Mrs Chippy?'

'No, don't be daft McNish. The boy's a fantasist.'

McNish's expression sank, all hope draining away.

Sunil bent over and gingerly picked up the cat. Instantly the feline twisted so that he was the right way up, digging his claws into Sunil's shoulder while sniffing his ear. A deep purr vibrated through him.

Sunil got up and made for the tent entrance. Just as he was about to push through it, he felt a tug on his arm.

'You'll freeze.' It was Shackleton, trying to stop him. 'You've got no trousers on.'

'I'll be fine.' Sunil tried again to leave. A blast of cold air slunk into the tent. Mrs Chippy stopped purring.

'I won't let you hurt yourself!' Shackleton kept hold of his arm. 'You're part of the crew now and we are in this together.'

'Let go! I need to leave.' Sunil tugged his arm away. Mrs Chippy struggled in his arms.

'Let him go, Sir.' McNish grabbed Shackleton, who let go of Sunil in shock.

Sunil smiled. 'Good luck!'

He grabbed hold of the tent flaps and pulled himself out into the freezing air. His bare feet screamed in pain. Mrs Chippy's claws dug into Sunil's shoulder as he tried to climb out of his grasp and back into the warm tent. Sunil clasped Mrs Chippy tight. He glanced back into the tent to see both men staring, dumbfounded, as his bare feet left the ground. He hung in the air for a second and then **ZOOMED** up into the sky.

CHAPTER TWELVE

Sunil landed on Alex's roof. Mrs
Chippy wriggled free. For a moment
Sunil thought he had gone blind but
it was just the wool hat that they had
put on his head. He ripped it off and
threw it into the open skylight.

He looked over to Mrs Chippy. He looked like a startled owl. His fur glistened in the drizzle.

'It's OK,' Sunil said, offering a finger. But something else caught his eye. He glanced over the edge of the roof and his stomach dropped. He could see himself coming out of his own front door. He was moving awkwardly, trying to keep the broken record dry under his jacket.

His timeline had brought him back to earlier that day.

There was no tug on his belly button; he wasn't being kept in the past. The timeline itself must be confused as to when exactly he should be.

There was Mr Shaykes and his strange umbrella coming up to the front garden. That meant Alex herself would be landing on the roof at any moment.

'We can't be here,' Sunil whispered to Mrs Chippy.

Mrs Chippy didn't wait to be picked up. The moment he saw Sunil reach for him, he darted down the ladder in the skylight. Sunil was less nimble. He only just made it down to the ground when he heard the **WHUMP** of Alex landing on the roof.

He picked up the wool hat and
threw it into the living room. It
landed on top of the lobster tank.
Mrs Chippy had disappeared under
a sofa. Sunil would have to come
back for him later. He ran back
through the kitchen, carefully
squeezed past the manuals by the
back door. He was in his t-shirt and
pants with no shoes. Instead of going
through the brambles, he climbed up
a tree and carefully lowered himself

over the fence and down into his garden.

He opened the back door, told Tara to stop barking and ran upstairs to his bedroom. He crawled under his bed for his copy of *Great British Heroes from the Past* and looked in the index at the back for 'Shackleton'. He was outraged to find he wasn't listed. What did that mean? Had the men made it back? Did they all perish?

The back door slammed. His past self had come home. Moments later, the front door opened again. He slipped on a pair of tracksuit bottoms and crept out onto the landing. He heard his dad talking to a strange squeaky person. He didn't sound like that did he?! Sunil waited for Tara to be put on her lead and then crept downstairs as the front door shut. As he passed his dad's desk on the way to the kitchen, he spotted something. The *Wisden*

Cricketers' Almanack.[1] He picked it up and slipped his wellies on. He left via the back door, unlocking the gate at the back of the house. He noticed the wheelie bins weren't where they had been when he had used

1. *Wisden* (as it is known among cricket fans) is published every year in the UK. It was first published in 1864. It is known as the 'Bible of Cricket' but, to my knowledge, no one has ever used one to swear on in court.

them to climb over the fence so he moved them.

He retraced the route he and Alex had run to get away from Wiki.

CHAPTER THIRTEEN

Mr Shaykes was standing in the carpark, taking photos of himself. *What a show off*, Sunil thought. He wanted to slip inside the shop and get the *Antarctic Explorers* book he'd seen in the milkshake café's kitchen

but he couldn't get past while Mr
Shaykes was there. Sunil knew
Mr Shaykes would have to move
soon though because he was about
to meet Sunil and his dad in the
milkshake bar. Why wasn't he going
anywhere?

'Hey, Wiki!' Sunil shouted.

The kiwi **peeped** and Mr Shaykes
stopped taking photos.

'I'm the most interesting boy in
the world!' Sunil yelled across the

carpark. 'And I know all about your machine!'

Mr Shaykes looked confused and walked towards him. Sunil ran out of the carpark to the front of the shops.

'**STOP**!' Mr Shaykes said.

When Sunil got to the front of the café, he ducked behind the large 'we're open' street sign. He wasn't well hidden but he knew that Mr Shaykes would spot him inside the café.

Sure enough, moments later, Mr Shaykes rounded the corner and angrily entered the café.

Sunil snuck back past the shop front, catching a glimpse of himself being led by Mr Shaykes behind the counter to the kitchen. Now all he had to do was wait. He picked a spot in the car park, away from the white van he had hidden behind earlier, where he could still see the back door of the milkshake bar. His heart was hammering as he saw himself running out and hiding behind the van. Then out came Wiki, sniffing the air before running to the van and **peeping**. Out came Mr Shaykes with his net. Sunil saw himself run away followed by Wiki and Mr Shaykes. The coast was clear; Sunil took his chance and ran to the back door.

The kitchen was a mess. The Interesting Machine was still

churning milkshake out onto the floor. *Good thing I'm wearing wellies,* Sunil thought. He snatched up the *Antarctic Explorers* book from the windowsill. He was about to swap it for the *Wisden Cricketers' Almanack* when another thought occurred to him. He went over to the Interesting Machine and dropped the almanack into its object drawer.

CHAPTER FOURTEEN

The kitchen door was shut so Sunil banged on it. It was opened by the teenage girl from earlier. She looked confused.

'Where is Mr Shaykes?'

'Your machine is broken,' Sunil said, moving past her. 'He's gone for some spare parts.'

She looked into the kitchen. The machine was already puffing out brown smoke as it tried to digest an entire book of cricket statistics.

'Sunil?' said Dad.

'I think we should go home,' Sunil said.

'Yeah,' said the girl. 'I'm closing the shop.'

'Oh, that's a shame. Come on then, Tara,' said Sunil's dad.

They stepped outside. As the girl locked up, there was a massive **BANG**. The Interesting Machine had exploded. Milkshake was plastered over every window and oozed out of the gaps.

'How did you get here?' Mr Shaykes walked up behind them, pointing his net at Sunil. He turned on the girl. 'Don't gawp. Mop this up!'

The girl looked at him like he
was mad. 'I quit.'

'Come on, Dad,' Sunil said,
watching Mr Shaykes open the door
and get covered in milkshake. 'I
want to go home and read this.'

'*Antarctic Explorers…* is that
Scott and Shackleton?'

'You've heard of Shackleton?'
Sunil said as they started to
walk home.

'Yeah, wasn't his ship called the
Endurance?'

'Yes! Do you know what happened to them?' Sunil asked.

Sunil's dad murmured in the way grown-ups do when they don't know anything and started to whistle.

As they approached the house, they saw a kerfuffle in Alex's front garden. Tara barked. Alex stood between Mrs Chippy and Wiki, trying to keep them apart. Wiki was sniffing excitedly at Mrs Chippy and Mrs Chippy was swiping at the bird when it got too close.

'How did you get there?' Alex asked Sunil.

'We were going for milkshakes but there was an accident in the kitchen…' Sunil's dad explained. 'Have you got a cat now?'

'Oh yes, Dad, didn't I say? Alex got a cat called Mrs Chippy,' Sunil said.

'Did I?' Alex said angrily.

'Wait, isn't that that kiwi?' said Sunil, quickly.

At that moment Tara barked again, and jumped over the fence at the front of Alex's house, pulling Sunil's dad so he was bent over it. He dropped the lead and all the animals darted for each other. Fortunately, Wiki recognised the danger and sped away with Mrs Chippy in hot pursuit.

Sunil helped his dad back onto his feet, and called Tara over.

They heard a muffled voice from inside the house. 'What lovely claws you have!'

'Who's that?' Sunil's dad asked.

'You have a gorgeous beak,' the robotic voice of BM said as Alex slid through the door.

'OK, thank you, bye now!' Alex said, slamming the door shut.

'Strange lady.' Sunil's dad opened the front door. 'Where are you going?'

'Upstairs to read my book!'

'Don't you want to play on the computer?'

'No thanks!' said Sunil.

He ran up to his bedroom and quickly went straight to the back pages of the book and looked up 'Shackleton'.

The evening grew darker as he learnt what happened to the crew of the *Endurance*. The silly book didn't mention Mrs Chippy. As the smell of his dad's cooking crept up the stairs, Sunil read how they walked for days but the ice kept dragging them back. They had only just made it to Elephant Island with no hope of rescue, when Sunil heard his mother shriek from the living room.[1]

1. They walked across and camped on the sea ice until it melted. Then they rowed the lifeboats to the uninhabited Elephant Island, reaching it on April 16th 1916. After recovering from that epic journey, Shackleton left most of the crew behind, took a small lifeboat and went to find help on April 24th 1916. Sixteen days after setting out, travelling 750 miles, he reached South Georgia island. He then trekked to a whaling station with the small group of men he had taken with him, to organise a rescue effort. On August 30th 1916, Shackleton returned to Elephant Island and rescued the remaining crew members. Incredibly, all the crew members survived!

'Who wrote "Neil Armstrong was here" on Grandad's record?!'

Sunil was in big trouble. **MASSIVE** trouble. The **BIGGEST** trouble any boy had ever been in.

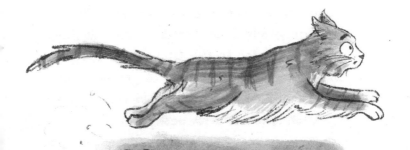

Look out for Sunil and Alex's
other adventures...

OUT NOW!

Alex's time machine is behaving strangely
and using it has become unpredictable
and dangerous. From the dark and gloomy
Tower of London to the tropical Galápagos,
will Sunil and Alex be able to get home in
one piece? And can they avoid the sinister
Mr Shaykes and his pesky pet kiwi?!

**MORE TIME MACHINE
NEXT DOOR ADVENTURES
COMING IN 2024!**

For information about more
historical fiction books
from Bloomsbury
visit www.bloomsbury.com.